Meet Some of the Men
Who Inspired My Book

"Yolanda, why are you so upset? The label said 'Wash with like colors.' My jeans are blue, your shirt was blue. It was silk? Gosh. Maybe you should do the laundry from now on."

—Melvin

"It's that time of the month again, isn't it, Yolanda?"

—Anthony

"Calm down, Yolanda, we're not lost. We're definitely not lost. I've driven through this neighborhood a thousand times . . . . Say, this intersection didn't used to be here."

—Eugene

"Yolanda, I introduced you to my parents as my friend because I think of you as a friend. A really good friend. You're a girl, and you're my friend. They know you're a girl, so I just say 'friend.' "

—Fritz

"Happy birthday, Yolanda!
Two tickets to the Knicks!"

—Tyrone

"Was it my fault they scheduled the amateur
softball league playoffs the same day as our
two-month anniversary? Hey, at least I left
you a note."

—Clyde

"Yolanda, you are one aggravated woman."

—Steven

HOW TO AGGRAVATE A WOMAN EVERY TIME . . .

HOW TO AGGRAVATE A WOMAN EVERY TIME . . .

& send her screaming out the door!

A BOOK FOR WOMEN
and the Men Who Annoy Them

YOLANDA I. HATEM

NEW YORK

Library of Congress Cataloging-in-Publication Data

Hatem, Yolanda I.
    How to aggravate a woman every time—and send her
screaming out the door! : a book for women and the men who
annoy them / by Yolanda I. Hatem.
        p.   cm.
    ISBN 1-56282-841-X
    1. Men—Humor. 2. Women—Humor. 3. Interpersonal
relations—Humor. 4. American wit and humor. I. Title.
PN6231.M45H35   1993
305.3'0207—dc20   92-38377
                                                  CIP

Design & Production by Robert Bull Design

FIRST EDITION

10 9 8 7 6 5 4 3 2 1

To Women, who love Men . . .
who aggravate Women . . .
who love Men . . .
who aggravate Women . . .
who love Men . . .

Contents

Introduction

WARNING

To the Reader:

The following information is highly sensitive.

If you are a man, you'd better sit up on the couch and maybe turn down the TV a little. While you're at it, go for another beer. Frankly, you're in for quite a shock.

If you are a woman . . . well, even you might be surprised at just how bad things have become.

LET'S FACE IT: **Women today are aggravated**. In these high-tech, high-pressure times, few women can get through the day without encountering *some* form of aggravation. It's worse now than ever before!

But do you know where that increase in aggravation has been most significant? *In women's romantic relationships with men*. Here are the results of a recent informal survey:

486 out of **500** women said they *regularly* had to put down the seat.

451 out of **500** women said their men *always* wore thick white sweat socks—even to go out to dinner.

500 out of **500** women said they were *constantly* aggravated by men.

Having spent many a night myself in the wet spot, I know *exactly* what these women mean when they say they're aggravated.

I've been greeted in the morning by beard stubble and toothpaste globs all over my sink and an empty juice container in the fridge, and I've been welcomed with those three little words every woman waits all day to hear from her man: "What's for dinner?"

I've been told that discussing birth control before sex is inappropriate because "it will ruin the illusion." I've been told the only reason people get married is to have children. I've been told "big breasts don't matter," only to witness the opposite.

In short, like most women I know, I've been underappreciated, underestimated, and I've even been pre-empted—by the World Series. That's why I've decided to put together the ultimate exposé of the male mind and its devious machinations: *How to Aggravate a Woman Every Time . . . and send her screaming out the door!*

The explicit information I've compiled here is not meant to harm anyone. As I've often been told, "It's nothing personal." My motives are simple: no one knows aggravation like I, Yolanda I. Hatem, know aggravation.

If my special insight into the bewildered, remote-control clicking male species can make people laugh, great. And if one man out there reading this suddenly wakes up and makes the coffee—not just smells it, and not just asks why there isn't any more—well, then, we'll all be a little less aggravated.

Y. I. Hatem

HOW TO
AGGRAVATE
A WOMAN
<u>EVERY</u> <u>TIME</u> . . .

Courtship

Return her phone calls after a delay—if at all—to show her who's in charge.

When you do call her, don't feel obligated to stop talking with whoever is in the room with you. Provide her the luxury of listening to your half of an ongoing conversation.

Call her answering machine and leave a message for an old girlfriend by mistake.

Get angry if her line is busy and you can't get through when you call. Then get even angrier when she finally gets call waiting—and puts you on hold.

When sandwiched up against a beautiful woman in a crowded public place, slyly cop a feel.

Always wear thick white sweat socks—even with your black dress shoes.

Wear knee socks with sandals.

Fix your broken glasses with duct tape and wear them in public.

Hit her with the best-friend syndrome: "I can't talk to anyone like I can talk to you."

Hit her with the second stage of the best-friend syndrome: "I just don't think about you in that way."

When she asks what you're doing over the weekend, mumble something about going out with friends and don't specify with whom.

When you're visiting and her phone rings, ask accusingly, "Who could *that* be?"

Consistently arrive fifteen minutes late to pick her up, then get angry the one time she needs a few extra minutes.

Never show up where and when you say you will.

Don't keep any of your promises to her.

Take her to an expensive restaurant for nouvelle cuisine and complain loudly about the portions when the food arrives.

Take her to *any* expensive restaurant and eat as though it's your first meal in weeks.

Get bent out of shape when she offers to pay the check.

If she has cats, say you're a "dog person."

If she has a dog, say you're a "cat person."

Keep a framed picture of your old girlfriend prominently displayed in your house.

Claim ignorance in bedmaking, ironing, cooking, and cleaning.

Say you don't want to talk about birth control because it will "ruin the illusion."

☎

During those first few moments of intimacy, when she asks if you have protection and you don't, lie. She won't mind once things get going.

☎

Try to shove your tongue down her throat on your first kiss.

☎

Stake your claim: leave a "love bite" high up on her neck or some other noticeable place.

☎

Don't stay the night.

☎

Spread rumors that she's sleeping with you when she's not.

☎

Spread rumors that she's not sleeping with you when she is.

☎

When she stays over, wear the bathrobe your ex gave you.

☎

When you stay over, help yourself to anything in her bathroom, including her toothbrush and razor.

☎

Answer the phone at 6 A.M. when her mother calls.

☎

Conveniently take a vacation when she's moving into a new apartment.

☎

Ask her to help you pack when you move.

☎

Neglect to mention that you have a girlfriend.

☎

Neglect to mention that you have a boyfriend.

☎

Neglect to mention that you have children.

☎

Neglect to mention that you have a wife.

☎

Relationships
with Family
and
Friends

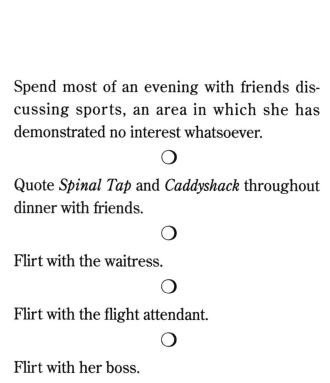

Spend most of an evening with friends discussing sports, an area in which she has demonstrated no interest whatsoever.

Quote *Spinal Tap* and *Caddyshack* throughout dinner with friends.

Flirt with the waitress.

Flirt with the flight attendant.

Flirt with her boss.

Flirt with her assistant.

○

Flirt with her sister.

○

Flirt with her mother.

○

Volunteer to watch the baby to allow her time to catch up with a friend. At a crucial point in their conversation, bring the baby into the room and announce, "Here, sweetheart, I think the baby has a dirty diaper."

○

Put her down in front of friends.

○

Say you're too tired to go shopping, but when your friends call, gleefully go out for a round of golf.

○

Criticize her mother.

○

Wear the outfit you know she hates when you meet her parents.

○

Forget or at least confuse the names of her family members and friends.

○

Refer to her as "my friend" or "my roommate" when introducing her to your family.

○

Never buy flowers for her, but be sure to send your mother an extravagant bouquet for Mother's Day.

○

Criticize her best friend.

○

Social Occasions

Argue with her about something trivial right before the dinner she's hosting, and sulk throughout the evening.

Don't bother telling her the party at your boss's house is semiformal.

Don't let her drive. If she insists, be a backseat driver.

Never, under any circumstances, allow her to navigate.

Refuse to stop and ask for directions even when you are hopelessly lost.

☿

Park in a handicapped spot: "They never check."

☿

Don't acknowledge her in public.

☿

Get lost when she takes you shopping at a mall.

☿

At the beach, offer to rub suntan lotion on her back. Spread it on in nifty patterns.

☿

Laugh when she's hit by a huge wave from behind and her swimsuit top falls down.

☿

In a restaurant, sit where you can see the TV.

☿

Tell the waiter you're both ready to order when she's not.

☿

Order for her at dinner without asking her what she'd like to eat.

☿

Don't hold her hand at the movies.

☿

Do laugh during all romantic scenes in movies. Tell her you thought *Ghost* was just plain stupid.

☿

Act insulted when she swoons over Mel Gibson in *Lethal Weapon*, then whistle loudly and wave at Michelle Pfeiffer during *Batman Returns*.

☿

Don't laugh at her jokes.

☿

Call her "the little woman."

♉

Call her "one of the boys."

♉

Ascribe political positions to her that she hasn't voiced herself.

♉

Interrupt her in the middle of a story and finish it yourself.

♉

Finish her sentences for her. That leaves more time for *you* to talk.

♉

Share a story about something great you did together, then, seeing her puzzled expression, say, "Oh, I guess that wasn't you after all."

♉

Repeat your stories many times over to the same people.

♉

24

When asked how you enjoyed your vacation, discuss the configurations of the plane you flew on.

♀

Be vague about your close relationships with other women, just to keep her guessing.

♀

Become very jealous when she talks to other men and insist that she stop.

♀

Get a crewcut—right before her college reunion.

♀

Make fun of her ex-boyfriends.

♀

Say "Just one more drink" long after it's obvious that your host and hostess want you to leave, or announce "We're going home" just as dessert is being served.

♀

Domestic
Life

Ask her to move in, then don't move any of your stuff to make room for hers.

◻▪

Surprise her by decorating the house: tack up your favorite posters from college, hang your tennis racket collection on the wall in a pleasing montage, buy wind chimes.

◻▪

Refuse to put out the picnic table until August, then don't put it back in the garage until December.

◻▪

Promise to paint the living room this week.

❑

Promise to paint the living room—next weekend.

❑

Promise to paint the living room "soon."

❑

Say, "Why go to all the trouble to paint the living room when you're just going to move eventually anyway?"

❑

Blame everything on an old knee injury.

❑

Renew your subscription to *Playboy*—and be sure to have at least one copy visible when her mother comes to visit.

❑

Refuse to get rid of all your *National Geographic*s from the 1950s.

❑

Refuse to let her put your high school wrestling trophies in the attic.

☐

Assure her periodically that you're going to clean out the garage. Then just rearrange the stuff in it.

☐

Refuse to decide which drill *really* works and throw away the other two.

☐

Refuse to throw away the unidentifiable metal object in the garage because "It might come in handy some day."

☐

Refuse to throw away the bell-bottom jeans in your closet. (Then wear them out one night as a groovy "surprise.")

☐

Even though they barely cover your navel, insist on wearing your old T-shirts from high school: "They still fit."

□⫶

Collect rubber bands, bread ties, and empty jars and then refuse to throw them away because "Who knows when we'll need them?"

□⫶

Keep all your old cans of tennis balls. When she insists they're flat, bounce one and say triumphantly, "There's a little life in it still!"

□⫶

Never throw *anything* away, especially old underwear—the more holes, the better.

□⫶

Challenge yourself: See how long you can go without changing your underwear.

□⫶

Insist on getting a pet. If this doesn't work, name all your plants.

□⫶

Talk to the dog instead of to her.

❏

Say, "The dog likes me better."

❏

When the dog barks at the neighbors and eats their garbage, say, "Maybe we should take *your* dog to obedience school."

❏

Pet the dog, play with the dog, give the dog treats. . . but never walk the dog or offer to clean up the lawn.

❏

Pet the cats, play with the cats, buy catnip-stuffed toys with bells. . . but never clean the litter box.

❏

After much nagging remember to pick up the dry cleaning, then toss it on the bed for the cats to sleep on.

❏

Ask, "Where's my wallet."

Ask, "Where are my keys?"

Ask, "Where's the remote."

Ask, "Where's my to-do list?"

Ask, "Where's the address book?"

Ask, "Where's the cat?"

But remember: When you're behind the wheel of a car, never, *ever* ask, "Where are we?"

Take up golf *before* you retire—and actually watch it on TV.

Refuse to read the instructions on any appliance; "Aw, c'mon, honey, any idiot can work one of *these!*" Then blame the manufacturer when it breaks.

☐

Lecture her about her compulsive clothes shopping, then go out and buy twenty CDs for yourself.

☐

Complain about her spending habits, but refuse to let her try to find a job.

☐

Offer unsolicited advice on balancing her checkbook.

☐

When you do go shopping, buy another pair of sneakers; you can never have too many.

☐

Put empty juice/milk/soda bottles back in the fridge: "I thought there was some more left."

☐

Buy frozen pizza, frozen burritos, potato chips, Cheez Whiz, and Oreos when it's your turn to get groceries.

❑❚

Drink orange juice right out of the container.

❑❚

Replace an empty ice cube tray in the freezer without putting water in it.

❑❚

Make coffee or tea for yourself in the morning, and leave the milk out when you're finished.

❑❚

Make coffee or tea for yourself in the morning, and put the milk back—in the cabinet.

❑❚

Be sure to greet her when she gets home from work with the three words no woman can hear often enough: "What's for dinner?"

❑❚

Eat an entire container of ice cream in one sitting.

❑▮

Watch whatever sports event is being broadcast while distractedly eating a meticulously prepared culinary feast.

❑▮

Plaintively ask if you can't have a steak when she presents you with a special gourmet meal.

❑▮

Actively discourage her from trying to share the meal she prepared for you.

❑▮

Pour salt and other unhealthy condiments all over the exquisite meals she cooks for you.

❑▮

Ask her to make you apple pie like your mom used to make, then grimace after tasting it.

❑▮

Say her cooking is not quite as good as your mother's.

❑▤

Say her cooking is not anywhere near as good as yours—but you're too busy to cook.

❑▤

Leave your dirty dishes in the sink, then when she starts washing them, say, "Oh, I was going to do those!"

❑▤

Insist on using the good guest towels in the bathroom when there is always a clean but less fluffy towel to use hanging behind the door.

❑▤

Then use the decorative hand towels to clean your feet.

❑▤

Leave the toilet seat down—and don't aim.

❑▤

Make sure there's always plenty of dirty laundry. Change clothes at least three times a day—even after wearing a shirt for only an hour, be sure to stuff it in the hamper. (This is much easier than folding it up and replacing it in the drawer.) It also helps to use a new towel every time you shower.

☐

When showering, leave the bath mat hanging in the shower.

☐

Leave the toilet seat up, especially during the night—she's more likely to fall in that way.

☐

Leave one piece of toilet paper on the roll.

☐

Splash water everywhere when shaving in the sink.

☐

Never rinse away toothpaste scum.

☐

Leave a thick tangle of hair on the soap.

☐

Leave beard stubble all over the bathroom sink, toothbrushes, toothpaste tube, and mirror.

☐

Lavishly splash on her $50 astringent (skin-cleansing lotion) as a refreshing after-shave.

☐

Leave your wet towel on the bed.

☐

Holidays
and
Anniversaries

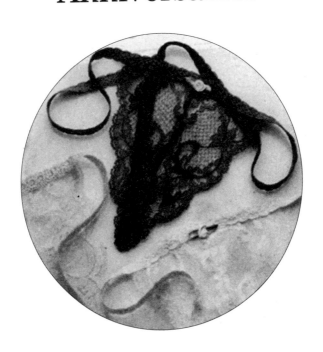

Buy her X-rated lingerie for Valentine's Day—four sizes too small.

Buy her X-rated lingerie for Valentine's Day—four sizes too large.

For her birthday each year, continue to buy her variations of the clever T-shirt she was so enthusiastic about the first time you presented it.

For her birthday, buy her tickets to your favorite sports event.

For any special occasion, get her a present you really want for yourself.

Buy her a birthday present at the airport after returning from a business trip.

Even though you know exactly what she wants for her birthday, get her something you're *sure* she'll like better.

Arrange to go play pool with your friends on her birthday.

Forget to acknowledge Valentine's Day.

Forget your wallet when you go out for an anniversary dinner.

Forget your anniversary.

Forget which day her birthday is, then send a belated greeting with a sorrowful-eyed kitten on it.

Use the vacation money you've both been saving to buy a laserdisc player.

Use the money you were saving for an engagement ring to "invest" in a boat: "We can go sailing on our honeymoon!"

Romantic Moments

Record your relationship for posterity: Take her picture when she least expects it, like the first thing in the morning or as she steps out of the shower.

Make fun of her screaming about a spider in the bathtub, and refuse to squish it.

Spend an hour talking with friends on the phone, then when she wants to talk, say you're tired and want to watch television.

When watching TV, proudly display your digital dexterity by clicking the remote control nonstop.

Turn on a football game just as she's settled down to read a good book.

Take her book out of her hand to see what she's reading—and lose the page.

Stick your smelly feet in her lap when she's trying to read the paper and ask for a foot rub.

When she's happily immersed in her favorite sitcom, walk in and change the channel, proclaiming, "There's a great documentary you've got to see!"

Ask, "Do you feel like Chinese food?" Then wait for her to get up and order it.

Say you're not hungry—then gaze longingly at the pizza slice she went out to get, until she gives it to you.

Constantly ask for a back rub and never offer one.

Promise you'll give her a back rub if she gives you one first. Then promptly fall asleep when your back rub's finished.

Turn white at the mention of marriage.

Tell her you want to get married. . . you just don't know when.

Tell her you want to get married . . . when business is better.

Tell her you want to get married . . . maybe next year.

Tell her the only reason people get married is to have children.

Tell her she doesn't know what she's talking about.

Don't listen to her when she's talking.

Yawn when she's trying to discuss a serious relationship matter with you.

Ask how her day was, then interrupt her and tell her how your day was.

Ask how her day was, then go into the next room.

Don't ask how her day was.

Don't trust her instincts.

Expect applause for doing things she does every day without any.

Talk baby talk to her when she's in a bad mood.

Look at her blankly when she tells you she loves you.

Say, "I told you so," in any context.

"Accidentally" read her diary, then confront her about some of the contents.

Sulk, and when she asks, "What's wrong?" say, "Nothing."

When she knows that you know that she knows that something is bothering you, still say, "Nothing."

When she stops asking "What's wrong?" act hurt and tell her she doesn't seem to care at all about your feelings.

Act like nothing is wrong after a big fight. Say, "Wanna go to a movie?"

Send flowers and think everything's all better.

Invite several friends over and play loud music when she's in bed with cramps on a Saturday.

Try for the opposite extreme: Calendar her menstrual cycle so you can be "prepared" for PMS.

When she says she wants to talk, automatically assume she's having PMS.

Always attribute any aberration in her behavior to PMS.

When she craves her PMS chocolate chip cookies, suggest she have celery to "help her on her diet."

When she is trying to diet, tell her, "You look just right, honey, go ahead and have dessert." Then, later, tease her about not fitting into last year's shorts.

When she's sticking to her diet and you're out on the town together, be sure to order her favorite dessert for yourself.

Recommend your ex-girlfriend's exercise class to her.

Buy her a "Buns of Steel" workout tape.

Buy her the Cindy Crawford workout tape for your own viewing pleasure.

Kid her about gaining 5 pounds—after you've just put on an extra 25.

Lose weight faster than she does. After all, you don't have to fight the female fat cell.

Be fooled by other women's "natural" look.

Tell her she doesn't need any makeup and that she looks beautiful without it—even though you've never seen her without it.

Try to have a longer ponytail than she does.

When she has her hair cut 6 inches shorter, mention for the first time how much you *love* long hair.

Fail to notice her new hairstyle.

Gloat over the fact that you never have a bad hair day.

Always try to avoid telling an outright lie. When she asks if it looks as though she's gained weight, say, "No, not really."

When she asks how her dress looks, say, "Fine," without lifting your eyes from the TV.

When you do lift your eyes from the TV, say, "Oh, is *that* what you're wearing?"

Suggest that maybe she's too old to wear minis.

Suggest that maybe she might find a one-piece bathing suit more comfortable.

Say you really don't mind the fact that she doesn't have big breasts—then ogle every big-breasted woman who walks by.

As you fondle her breasts during an intimate moment, murmur in her ear: "Ah, the smaller the grapes, the sweeter the wine."

Tell her you're not impressed by gorgeous, slender glamour girls—you'd rather come home to *her*.

Give her other backhanded compliments, such as "Black is so slimming," or "Your skin has really cleared up."

Ask if she dyes her hair.

Compare her to your ex-girlfriend: "You know, honey, *Amy* never minded when I didn't shave."

Say you'd be happy to discuss her concerns if only you understood what they were.

The Bedroom

Occasionally have too much to drink and pass out fully clothed next to her in bed before you've barely kissed her goodnight.

Every night, sort out your change in excruciatingly exact rows on the dresser while she waits for you to come to bed.

Insist on keeping the alarm clock on your side of the bed, then sleep through the alarm, knowing she can't reach it.

Whether you actually did or not, assure her that you set the TV timer before climbing into bed. (Lay low when she gets up at 3 A.M. to turn off the set.)

Leave your underwear on the floor, then say, "This place is a mess!"

Require eight pillows, then steal hers while she's sleeping.

Steal the sheets.

Sleep with your arms around her like an octopus, so when she wakes up, her whole body has gone to sleep.

Complain that you can't sleep when she's using the night–light to read.

Keep the night-light on to read when she wants to sleep.

▭

During foreplay, press on and around a random part of her lower anatomy and ask, "Is this it?"

▭

Silently rub a random part of her lower anatomy in the false assumption that it is "it."

▭

Push her head down to indicate you'd like a blowjob.

▭

Coax her into giving you a blowjob, but don't return the favor.

▭

Perform oral sex until she starts to get interested, then stop and tell her you're so excited you can't wait any longer.

▭

Call out another woman's name at the moment of climax.

Call out a man's name at the moment of climax.

Call out any name other than hers or God's at the moment of climax.

Take it personally if she doesn't come every time.

Take it personally if she doesn't come more than once every time.

Turn on the TV, light up a smoke, poke around in the refrigerator, or fall into a deep sleep immediately afterward.

Make sure *she* always gets to sleep in the wet spot.

If it was all over in 30 seconds or less, dare to ask, "Was it good for you?"

If All Else Fails...

Hold up a copy of *How to Aggravate a Woman Every Time . . . and send her screaming out the door!* and say, "Honey, I don't do any of these things, do I?"

Acknowledgments

Yolanda I. Hatem is grateful to Jenny Gauthier and Mary Ann Naples for their editorial suggestions and enthusiasm for this project.

Thanks also to Christy Archibald, Christina Arneson, Wesley Bassett, Susan Brogan, Leslie Brooks, Carla Byrnes, David Cohen, Ellen Cowhey, Victoria DiStasio, Peggy Garry, Marcy Goot, Adrian James, Linda Kaplan, Lisa Kitei, Kris Kliemann, Lesley Krauss, Jennifer Landers, Bridget Levy, Clio Manuelian, Michelle Maryk, Tom Miller, Pat Mulcahy, Carol Perfumo, Linda Prather, Liz Rabinowicz, Judith Riven, Carol Smith, Vincent Stanley, Victor Weaver, Leslie Wells, Audra Zaccaro.

And a big thanks to my empathetic publisher, Bob Miller. Long before reading the manuscript, he knew how to make the coffee.